really need

Condition 1: Santa's Quality Presents Company will respond to orders placed by the Party of the Second Part [henceforth referred to as "The Customer"] in either a) traditional methods of letters up a chimney or visits to a sanctioned 'Santa' or b) modern use of email or via internet site.

Condition 2: The Party of the Second Part [henceforth referred to as 'The Santa'] will be making a list and thence be checking it twice, for the purposes of determination as to who has been either naughty or nice.

Condition 3: Requests for rooftop or stockinged deliveries will no longer be fulfilled [following prohibitive increases in roof landing indemnities]. Traditional Gratuities [carrots, mince pies, brandy etc.] will therefore no longer be expected, although will no doubt still be appreciated by any delivery men.

ISBN: 978-0-244-32039-3

11,973/10,000

Quality Presents

Christmas gifts you really need

Seasonal Shorts by
David J Brown

Contents

5. A gift of quality 7

4. Gift Exchange 20

3. Denial of Service 35

2. A gift of time 50

1. A Present for Santa 69

Appendix A – Article 83

Appendix B – Begging Questions 85

Appendix C – Commercialism and Charity 87

Santa's Quality Presents

Christmas gifts you really need

5. A gift of quality

You would like Graham. You would like how he smiled as he held a door open for you.

Graham was a good boy. Not outstanding, but at least consistently good.

He *must* have been – how else would he have received at least one present from Father Christmas, every one of his twenty-two Christmases to date?

So, when this particular parcel arrived, a full week early, Graham knew that he shouldn't open it until the 25th. He did however remove it from its postal packaging, in search of any sender's information.

The parcel inside was wrapped in shiny red paper with the words 'Season's Greetings' printed regularly across it. He could hold it comfortably in one hand; giving it a quick heft, he thought he could sense something wobbling inside. This made him smile and he wanted to know who it was from, but there was no card fixed on the outside of the wrapping, no delivery invoice in the box.

'There's probably a card inside,' he thought, putting the gift on the floor where his little tree was due to go and out of his mind until Christmas.

He barely thought about that parcel over the next few days. He noticed it up on the shelf once or twice while he was watching television but wasn't tempted to open it early.

For a single young man, living in a small flat on his own, the final week of advent didn't seem at all special to Graham. It mainly revolved around gadget malfunction.

On Sunday he tried to put his little tree up but the instructions were only in Finnish, so he settled for draping tinsel over the chairs instead.

On Monday afternoon, he blocked the photocopier but couldn't find all of the pieces of shredded paper amongst its workings. Embarrassed and not wanting to make his mistake public, he spent three or four minutes trying to find them before giving up and leaving it for the next person to worry about.

On Tuesday morning, he saw Verity at the photocopier. She was a little blonde sparrow of a girl, always so determined and optimistic about things, but always on the *other* side of the room. He had found himself thinking about her a lot recently and, right now, he thought that he would ask her out.

She seemed to have opened every door and pulled out every possible tray and roller and was now referring to annotations on her phone, as it suggested solutions. She looked up at him from amongst the copier's innards. "Sorry Graham, what did you say?"

"I said, I wondered if you'd be free to go for a drink after work tomorrow? You know... breaking up for Christmas and everything?"

She looked deep into the heart of the copier, then to the diagnostic app on her phone, then back up at him. (He thought her eyes looked beautiful, looking up at him in that slightly defocussed way. He felt confident that she would say yes.)

"Sorry, no," she said. "There's something I have to do, tomorrow. Perhaps...."

"Okay, never mind," Graham said, slightly too soon, then quickly walked back to his desk.

That evening, he missed his bus home; only by a few seconds, but that was all it took. He sat on the bus stop seat for forty-five minutes, enjoying the sight of the world getting ready for Christmas around him.

On Wednesday, he played Angry Birds once. He couldn't get the last two pigs, so he thought it was probably too difficult for him and tried to delete it from his phone. It wouldn't uninstall though, so he settled for removing the icon.

Thursday was a day off, which he spent some of trying to wrap presents. He wasn't any good at wrapping though and, after fighting against the Sellotape dispenser over the first parcel, he moved over to using gift bags instead. When he ran out of gift bags, he finished with carriers.

Friday was Christmas morning. Graham got out of bed soon after ten and began the countdown to 'Church with his Mum', which would be followed by lunch at her house. (He was, as has already been noted, a good boy.)

He opened the three cards that had arrived and then turned his attention to the present that had sat there mostly unconsidered for a week. The sticky tape was a little too firm and thorough and he soon gave up scratching at it with his fingertips.

Once again, he felt that weird wobble within as he put it back on the shelf before he went back to brush his teeth.

But, while he was brushing, he could almost still feel the wobbling sensation from inside the box. It nagged at him, so he returned to the parcel with curiosity, renewed vigour and a small kitchen knife.

The tape slit open easily and he pulled a clear plastic box from its wrappings, staring at its contents in disbelief. Was it a nodding dog? Yes... a nodding dog! (A bulldog perhaps? He'd never learned names of dog breeds.) He took it out and sat it on his table.

Weren't you meant to put these in your car? He didn't have a car – why would someone give him this? Who would give him something like this?

Then he looked for any sign of who it was from. Nothing – just a little card from the company, with a brand name (Santa's Quality Presents) and a little explanation:

```
The nodding dog of perseverance:
          "doggedness".
```

A while ago at the office he had overheard about Shirley, one of the receptionists, being given "seduction", which he assumed was probably a new brand of perfume. But perseverance? Why would someone want to give him perseverance? He gave it a sniff; it wasn't perfume. It was a dog that kept nodding at him.

There were no clues, no answers to be found, so he gave up.

He sat the card under the dog, on the table, and went out to his Mum's.

By lunch time on Boxing Day, Graham had written all of his thank you letters except one, the one for the nodding dog.

His Mum had taught him that, whatever he thought of a gift, he should always say thank you. He usually managed to get all of his thank you letters written before the year ended, so he would have to get on with finding out who sent the nodding dog. But he had no ideas how to do this.

The dog just sat on the table and nodded at him.

He was due back at work on Tuesday morning. After a bleary breakfast with the nodding dog, Graham stepped out of his flat a little late and watched his bus go past. Determined not to be late for work on his first day back, he ran down an alley to catch it at the next stop.

Back at home that night, he found himself sitting in front of the nodding dog, once again. It prompted him to think: Who could have sent the present? Someone with a sense of humour, presumably, who wanted him to laugh? He rang his mum.

"Hello Mum."

"Hello Graham. I got your thank you letter already. You are a good boy."

"Thanks Mum. Look, someone sent me a nodding dog for Christmas, but the card must've fallen off, so I don't know who to thank."

"Oh, that's embarrassing," his mother agreed.

"You don't know who sent it, do you?"

"Sorry love, no. I can't think who it might have been."

"So how can I say thank you?"

"Well love, I don't see how you can. Well, I suppose you shouldn't just give up." That was how well she knew him. "Have you thought of anyone who usually sends you a present but hasn't, this year?"

Graham put down the phone and looked at the nodding dog. It was gently encouraging him with its nodding. He would definitely like to say thank you and decided at that moment that he would not give up.

On Wednesday, while trying to help Shirley catch up with her work, he blocked the photocopier again. He had a couple of goes at unblocking it; pulled out a couple of trays and spun some rollers, but couldn't find the offending paper.

Sitting across the office, he saw Verity at her desk. She'd be able to help him.

"Verity, have you still got that photocopier app on your phone?"

She looked over and smiled, "You know how I love my apps."

"I've blocked the copier again...," he said as he crossed the room to her.

"Oh, I suppose you want me to fix it for you, then?" She rolled her eyes and her chair back and stood up.

"No," he surprised himself by saying, "but I'd appreciate your help with doing it."

So, Verity unlocked her phone and found the app as they walked together back to the copier.

A couple of minutes later; a couple of failed attempts; a couple of mistakes and laughs... and they had it fixed. It was probably the longest they had ever spent talking, he reflected.

As she went back to her work, Graham found himself thinking, 'what a shame she didn't want to go out with me....' Instead though, he called across, "I'd like that app for myself... where did you get it from?"

"I'll send you the link," she smiled and opened up her phone's contact list. "Give me your number, then."

That night, he sat staring into the face of the nodding dog. If it hadn't been from his family,

15

it must have been sent by one of his friends. He would have to text them all to ask them. He got out his phone to draft the message. Seeing that he had been sent that link from Verity, he added her number to his contacts list before carrying on.

He didn't have very many friends, but getting them all to answer his texts took a while. One of them had heard of something like his dog (something like, was it... an owl that helped you to stay up late?), but swore that he hadn't sent it himself.

Disappointedly dropping his phone on to the table, he set the dog's smiling head nodding again. "You're right," he said to it. "There must be a way to find out."

The dog smiled back and nodded supportively.

Thursday was New Year's Eve. In the morning, he blocked the copier yet again and remembered to open the text from Verity, containing the link for the app. It wasn't the usual AppShop site; he recognised almost none of the apps there. After browsing for a minute however, he noticed a logo that looked familiar – the same 'Season's Greetings' design as on the wrapping paper of the nodding dog.

Oh... Verity...? She had been sitting across the room from him, all of this time!

How could it have been sent by Verity? A girl who hardly ever spoke to him... or was it that he hardly ever spoke to her? It was difficult to tell.

She would have used this app to order the gift for him, of course. She loved her apps, after all, didn't she?

But why would she have sent it? She wasn't interested in him... hadn't she already turned him down when he had asked her, that once?

Sitting back at his desk, he realised that he was smiling broadly and nodding his head, just like the little dog was probably doing right now, at home. Maybe asking once wasn't enough... maybe he shouldn't have given up that easily. Maybe he should try asking her again? He took a deep breath, stood up and walked across to her desk.

"Verity?"

She looked up; not surprised... perhaps relieved?

"Verity, would you like to go out tonight... to welcome in 2016?"

She smiled broadly and nodded. "I'd love to. Although, it won't be easy to get tickets, at this notice."

"No… but I promise you I won't give up before I get some." His head nodded up and down rhythmically, with a big smile that wouldn't leave his face.

4. Gift Exchange

As a younger girl, Jodie had written to Father Christmas every year. Only once had she got what she asked for... and that had turned out to be part-coincidence, part-mistake.

Truth be told, more often than not she had misplaced the letter and never sent it. This was one of the reasons why she had taken to buying presents for herself, while finding them for everyone else. That and, when December came and family began to ask, she could never find the lists she had made of what she wanted.

But she did care about doing Christmas well. One year she had passed a shop, late at night, and had seen the perfect wrapping paper in the window. It was pale, with almost ghostly imprints of Victorian street maps printed across it in pastel shades. Jodie had never really gotten on with maps, but she found this design fascinating and beautiful. She had stared at it for drunken minutes, vowing to return and buy it the next weekend, but never managed to find the shop again.

After that night, whenever she tried to look for the shop or the wrapping paper, her boyfriend Paul thought she was wasting her time; he didn't care or understand why she would care that much about sheets of wrapping. "The paper doesn't matter. It's what's inside that counts," he would say.

But Jodie thought that it did matter. It mattered to her, anyway.

People at the warehouse she worked in understood her much better. They had even put coloured arrows on the ground at key junctions to help her to find the way back to her office.

One February, a guy she had fancied for ages (Italian, artistic, attentive, fork-lift driver) had given her a Valentine's card in an envelope printed with a familiar pattern of Victorian streets, printed in pinks and reds. Inside was an invitation and his phone number... which she had then put somewhere so safe that she could never find it again. He had left the warehouse, later that spring.

Tonight, Jodie wanted to relax, but didn't feel ready to go into the lounge yet. She was still smarting from the great sofa debacle: on delivery, they couldn't get it in through the door, so they had dismantled it on the pavement, then carried it in and rebuilt it in the lounge, where it turned out to be too big – either obstructing the doorway or half of the television.

Paul really liked the sofa though and didn't much care that Jodie had ordered one that didn't fit. Maybe in their next place it would fit okay? But Jodie was still annoyed with herself every time she saw it, so spent an increasing amount of time sitting with her laptop at the dining room table.

Fireworks Night was past; the shops were filling with Christmas, and Jodie with corresponding excitement. She began browsing for gifts, spent hours looking for just the right presents. Actually, she did this a little every year, but this year it seemed to be all that she did.

She found the size of the internet quite overwhelming. There were so many places you could go, interlinked in so many different ways that it never took her very long to get lost. She really wanted a map.

After half an hour trying to find her way back to the website where she'd seen some reliable shoes for her mother, Jodie found herself trapped in some sort of one-way-system of clickbait. Each page was overflowing with attractive pictures and enticing links, such as 'ten celebrities you never would believe haven't had plastic surgery'.

One such ad that caught her eye was 'Quality Presents you REALLY need!'. It looked a little naïve, but Jodie was in the mood for that sort of silliness. It took her to a web outlet containing a series of images advertising the strangest things: qualities... personal qualities for sale?

From a simple list, she selected bravery, with the icon of a lion – perhaps she would have expected to find a medal of a heart, but a lion made enough sense to her. Bravery, now that was a tempting idea...she would like to be braver. But no, she didn't really need it and certainly didn't believe in buying things you didn't need. She kept clicking.

Paul wandered past and into the kitchen. "Tea?"

"Thanks." He said something else but she couldn't hear him now, over the noise of the kettle. "What?"

He came back out. "You planning Christmas already?"

They drifted inexorably into the usual conversation about not wanting to spend Christmas Day with her parents again. He didn't care that it was her turn. He didn't notice how upset she was at his lack of understanding of her.

Paul said, "You got us lost, last time we went to my folks... we didn't get there till five. We owe them a proper day."

"But it's definitely my parents' turn for Christmas."

"Not by my accounting," he muttered as he went back into the kitchen.

Finding herself wishing that he would disappear, she searched the Quality Presents website for 'invisibility', but they didn't appear to do that. Although they did do the reverse... they did something to make yourself more visible to others. (Hi-vis underpants! Hilarious, she thought.)

Paul dropped her mug of tea off, then turned and disappeared back into the lounge.

"Thanks." Jodie could barely pull any attention away from that website.

She browsed further. Empathy... bubbliness... inspiration... none of these were what she needed (she wondered if she might benefit from some inspiration, but thought she could probably work it out for herself).

Spatial awareness…oh… that was it. That was what she needed. Oh, that was a shame: it was represented by a sliding puzzle; she had never been able to do those.

Paul walked in once more and tutted at her internet shopping, on his way to the toilet.

"I just can't understand why you waste your time like that. I always go to the shopping centre once, in the week before Christmas and don't come home until I've found something that would do for everyone."

Jodie didn't listen to his rant. Not just because she'd heard it all before… but because she was away on a thought train of her own.

He went back to the lounge, to watch the left half of Top Gear.

Reading a little more about it on the website, Jodie realised that she desperately wanted to buy some spatial awareness for herself. She was still bothered that it was represented by a sliding puzzle, but she could understand its totemic significance.

Clicking through to the online order form, she was surprised that it required her to enter a good deal of information about the person you were going to give the gift to, including an assessment of how good they'd been throughout that year (along with references who could support that.)

She filled in all of this for herself but when it came to putting her own details in for payment, it wouldn't accept them. A dig through the small print conditions eventually revealed that she couldn't send a gift to herself.

"How disappointing," she grumbled to herself. Paul just laughed at her frustration, from the other room. Why didn't he understand her? Why couldn't he be more sympathetic? 'Oh,' she thought, 'maybe what she would really like for Christmas was for Paul to understand her better?' Hadn't she browsed past sympathy a few minutes ago? No… maybe it was empathy… what was the difference between those again?

Maybe that would also be a present for them both… to make him sympathise better with her?

The website did sell both empathy and sympathy, she saw, but at first she couldn't decide which quality to buy for Paul. Did she want him to sympathise with her situation or empathise with her? She definitely wanted him to share her viewpoint sufficiently (and not only just so that he would then know to buy her the quality she wanted, in return).

Jodie reached for her dictionary to look them up. (She did know that she could just Google them, but she was worried that, if she left this webpage, she would never be able to find it again.)

Empathy - the ability to experience the feelings of another; also 'putting yourself in their shoes'.

Sympathy - caring and understanding for the misfortune of others.

'Empathy,' thought Jodie. 'I want Paul to be able to understand how I feel about things like this, not just feel sorry for me.'

This time the buying process went more smoothly, although the required pages of examples of his being 'good' throughout 2010 seemed a little excessive, and not always easy to complete with integrity. As she listed example after example of his behaviour, she felt pleased to see the informetric swing-o-meter settle clearly on the side of 'good'.

The parcel arrived on the last day of November. Jodie had locked herself out, had left her phone somewhere inside the house and had got herself lost coming back from the shops (just the usual shops, nowhere exotic). So, she happened to be standing on her doorstep as the package was delivered - and was still there hefting it when Paul got back home and let her in.

It wasn't a good time to tell Paul about her difficulties as he had spent his journey home getting increasingly angry about their bookshelves, all over again; ever since Jodie had ordered and built them, she had never been able to get things to fit satisfactorily (and there was no way that he was going to do it for her).

"If it wasn't for me, you'd have trouble finding your nose to pick it!" he said fondly, opening the front door and going in first.

Jodie took a deep breath, followed him through to the kitchen and handed him the parcel. "Merry Christmas!" she forced a smile.

"But it's not even December yet – or are you worried you'll lose it before Christmas?" he laughed, a little cruelly, this time.

"Open it. Go on."

He did as he was told. He opened the brown box to remove a shoe-box sized parcel, wrapped in shiny red paper with 'Season's Greetings' printed all over it.

She insisted he open it straight away, even though it was still very early to be giving Christmas presents.

"What is this? Old shoes?" (He ignored the little delivery card that fell out of the wrapping.) "What is it with you? What's wrong with normal presents?"

"They're someone else's shoes." She enjoyed his confusion.

"What? They're not even the right size."

"That's not the important thing. Try walking a little in them, please." He saw that this was an instruction, not a suggestion.

And so he did.

He felt slightly foolish when he went back out of the front door. Then he became amused as he turned onto the street. Then entertained as he passed a lamp post. Next, a little sad as he reached the corner of the road.

He couldn't believe the rush of emotions that ran through him. Finally, he walked back down the street and took the old shoes off when he reached the doorway. Almost cradling them in his arms, he understood why she had given them to him.

'What a gift!' he thought.

"You'd probably like a cup of tea now," he said.

That night, Paul sat at Jodie's computer after she had given up on the day and gone to bed. Holding the little delivery card that had dropped out of his present, he Googled the website and looked for something to buy her in return.

Now that he finally got her... that is, understood where she was coming from, he couldn't believe that it had taken him this long. What should he get for her? What did she really need?

Optimism? No, she had managed to remain overwhelmingly positive, despite what a git he had... often... been.

Spatial awareness? Perhaps? He looked up at their new shelves, so poorly, so inefficiently organised.

Bubbliness? She'd been a bit quiet recently, but he felt sure that she'd come back out of herself at Christmas – especially now that he could see where she was coming from; how it all fitted together for her.

Spatial awareness. That's what she really wanted. He understood that now. Clicking on the item, he saw that it was represented as a sliding puzzle.

The second parcel arrived just in time for Christmas, bearing a Finnish post mark. Paul laughed at the cheesiness of it, opened the outer box, took the red-wrapped parcel out and placed it under the tree with Jodie's other presents (none of which he had left until the last minute to buy, this year).

On Christmas Day, she wasn't at all surprised when she opened the parcel, but was both pleased and a little apprehensive. What if it didn't work for her, as it had for him? "Go on," he encouraged. "Have a go."

She started sliding the numbers around randomly, then saw how to get the 2 next to the 1... and then noticed that the 3 was nearby... and had all of the numbers in order within five minutes.

She carried it in her pocket to her parents' house and worked out how to make the numbers represent a derived Fibonacci sequence while she was laying the table. Her family laughed enthusiastically at Paul's shoes but did find him easier to get on with than ever before. "I think you've got to walk at least a mile in these old beauties before you really start to feel the benefit," he explained, sincerely.

On Boxing Day, Jodie was reorganising her bookshelves to make them both feel better.

Stowed safely inside an old copy of *Father Christmas*, by Raymond Briggs, she stumbled upon some old Christmas letters that she had lost before sending. Re-reading them, after all these years, she thought about how her wants had changed: from selfish and concrete to abstract and self-improving.

As she folded the envelopes carefully back together she thought that, at least this year, she had received the one present she really needed. With her newly improved spatial awareness, she could see exactly where she would be placing this book, in three shelves' time.

Moving to the next shelf that needed sorting, an old pink and red envelope fell out. Recognising the Victorian road map print immediately, she held her breath as she re-opened it. Of course, it was the lost Valentine's card from that lovely Italian fork-lift guy.

The next morning, Jodie went straight to the stationery shop that she'd discovered before and bumped into the Italian guy standing right next to the pale map wrapping paper, which she also really wanted.

She bought the wrapping paper, confident that she would still know where it was next December, to wrap Paul's present in.

David Brown

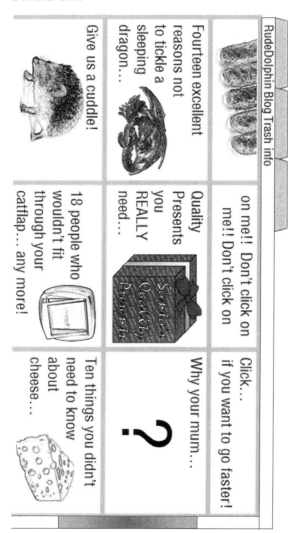

Fourteen excellent
reasons not
to tickle a
sleeping
dragon....

Give us a cuddle!

Quality
Presents
you
REALLY
need...

18 people who
wouldn't fit
through your
catflap... any more!

on me!! Don't click on
me!! Don't click on

Click....
if you want to go faster!

Why your mum....

?

Ten things you didn't
need to know
about
cheese...

34

3. Denial of Service

From: A. Abett
To: enquiries@QualityPresents.co.fi
23/11/2000 18:28

Dear Quality Presents Co.

I am writing to query the return of funds to my account, following the cancellation of an order I placed with you, in plenty of time for Christmas.

It was a potted bulb of "Common Sense" – some sort of narcissus, I believe?

The gift isn't for me, of course. It is for my wife who, I feel, is making increasingly strange choices, with wildly unrealistic expectations. I just need her to ground herself a little, so I was disappointed to receive the cancellation.

There was no message accompanying the cancellation. Perhaps it was due to a failed payment or your being out of stock of that particular item? If this was the case, then perhaps I could order the Kitchen Balance of Fairness instead? Possibly a more even-handed outlook would also help her?

I understand that, at this busy time of year, some small errors will be made and some stock will be sure to run out. However, perhaps I could request that your customer services department be alerted to this particular oversight, in order to avoid such errors in the future?

Yours faithfully
Aidan Abett

- - - - - - - - -

Junior Partner, Smann, Ropend and Abett
Better than you because we care just enough.

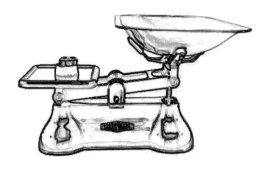

From: Quality Presents
To: A.Abett@DingbatMail.co.uk
24/11/2000 09:03

Dear Mr Abett

We thank you for your communication of 23/11/2000. [Please be aware that we do not typically prioritise responding to emails, as our historical policy favours hand-written letters to the boss.]
Referring back to your file, I can confirm that your order was cancelled from our end, following our regular data verification process.

Copied below is a brief summary of our conditions of sale and we have noted that your order contravenes condition two, hence voiding this purchase of a "Gift of Quality" from us.

Please do accept our sincere apologies for this inconvenience. We do hope that you can understand our own desire to maintain only the most deserving of client bases.

Sincerely yours,
Colin Elfsson
Customer Disservice Department

Condition 1: Santa's Quality Presents Company will respond to orders placed by the Party of the Second Part [henceforth referred to as "The Customer"] in either a) traditional methods of letters up a chimney or visits to a sanctioned 'Santa' or b) modern use of email or via internet site.

David Brown

Condition 2: The Party of the Second Part [henceforth referred to as 'The Santa'] will be making a list and thence be checking it twice, for the purposes of determination as to who has been either naughty or nice.

Condition 3: Requests for rooftop or stockinged deliveries will no longer be fulfilled [following prohibitive increases in roof-top indemnities]. Traditional Gratuities [carrots, mince pies, brandy etc.] will therefore no longer be expected, although will no doubt still be appreciated by any delivery men.

--*-*-*-*-*

Please consider the environment before taking up the euphonium.

From: A. Abett
To: enquiries@QualityPresents.co.fi
24/11/2000 13:11

Dear Mr Elfsson

Thank you for your prompt reply.

I was further disappointed to hear that you consider my wife to have been "not nice enough" over the past year. For all her faults, she is a fundamentally good person. In fact, the unrealistic projects I referred to in my previous email were almost exclusively for the benefit of others. Most recently, she thought she might be able to re-decorate our entire lounge while I was away on a stag weekend. (And she would have managed it too, if the lads and I hadn't returned earlier than expected to watch the match. Still, she replaced the furniture with good grace in time for kick-off and finished the painting the following weekend, of course.)

Perhaps I was a little cursory when completing your online order form? There are many good things that my wife, Megan, has done during this year which are worthy of recognition. Not only does she spend the majority of her time caring for our child, but she also manages to have my evening meal on the table every night, as I return from work.

She completes her allotted domestic chores in good time and consistently remains within her household budget. While the rugby or cricket is on,

39

David Brown

she will also take our child out of the house to minimise its distractions.

On Mothers' Day this year, she even managed to cook a three course Sunday luncheon for all three of our remaining parents, while I took the old man for a pint at the pub.

So, please do reconsider – and re-check her records. I assure you that she is worth the effort.

Sincerely
Aidan

- - - - - - - - -

Junior Partner, Smann, Ropend and Abett
Belittlement by proxy.

From: Elfsson, Quality Presents
To: A.Abett@DingbatMail.co.uk
25/11/2000 09:14

Dear Mr Abett

Please let me begin by assuring you that, having checked our 'behavioural informetrics' records, it is clear that your wife has been plenty good enough, this year. In fact, we would rank her within the thirtieth centile.

However, it is your own record that has fallen short during 2000, for the eighth consecutive year. Hence, a flag on your record tagged an automatic cancellation. I am afraid that we experience these so rarely that we have no established administrative procedure.

We would not normally release the following information, but as we consider yours a most special case, here is a brief selection from your personal records from the year 2000:

- Twenty three counts of ignorant selfishness.
- Forty three instances of unwarranted pride.
- Five separate insufferable whinges.
- Eighty three instances of unreasonable expectations.
- Failing to brush your teeth – once for three consecutive days.
- Frequent blaming of your faults on others (for your own records, we have found no enforceable precedent for assertion of the

link between the dealing of an act and the smelling of it).

- Four counts of falsely telling charity collectors that you 'give by standing order'.
- Fourteen occasions where you secretly ate too many sweets while failing to offer to share with others.
- Ninety two interruptions of Megan's phone calls for petty or otherwise minor demands.

We never intend to cause offence, but we do insist on maintenance of our high standards.

With continuing sincerity, and the best of luck with regular present purchasing in the remaining month,

Colin Elfsson
Behavioural Informetrics Division

*_*_*_*_*_*

You know how snowmen get to work, right?

From: A.Abett
To: enquiries@QualityPresents.co.fi
25/11/2000 13:11

Dear Mr Elfsson

I was grateful to receive your swift response to my previous email, although serially disappointed with its content. Please allow me now to make a detailed request to you to reconsider.

Here are some examples of my own recent 'good' behaviour:
Firstly, I give all of my old shoes to charity.
Secondly, I often hold doors open for anyone following me.
Thirdly, while driving, I only ever answer my mobile phone to really important calls.
Finally, I cycled for almost an hour in our company's charity "Tour de Office", in June.

My partners, Freya and Polly would most definitely provide references upon request. They see me as a very competent lawyer; good enough to have seen off all competition and make junior partner within five years.
As I suppose you must know, there was one minor 'naughty' deed, as you would call it. I know there was that one occasion where I sat in the reserved bus seating – but honestly, I didn't notice that woman was pregnant until I got off (I had thought that she was just fat – you would have too, if you had seen her, believe me!)

David Brown

If you do not find these points of positive evidence sufficiently 'good', I would formally request that this case be passed upwards to your manager.

Sincerely
Aidan

- - - - - - - - - -

Junior Partner, Smann, Ropend and Abett
Maintaining your subordination through superior education.

From: Colin Elfsson, Quality Presents
To: A.Abett@DingbatMail.co.uk
26/11/2000 09:29

Dear Mr Abett

Thank you once more for taking the time to communicate with us.

We do sincerely appreciate your concern for your classification on Mr Claus's database. As with all potential customers, we will undertake a thorough review of your behaviour over the next twelve months. In cases such as yours, we would not typically refer 'upwards' as you request, as He prefers to expend his valuable time on less unworthy issues.

Unfortunately, being described as a 'very competent lawyer' is not currently on our list of good behaviours (see below).

Mr Claus is keen that our customers do not behave well merely to qualify for our services, but most deeply believes one should be 'good for goodness's sake'.

For your information, we are currently considering the future launch of a new range of 'self-improvement' qualities for cases such as yours (e.g. the Threefold Mirror of Self-Reflection or the Porridge Oats of Restraint), but unfortunately these are not yet ready for the market.

In the meantime, here is a list of exemplary good behaviours which we maintain in the event of enquiries:

- Thanking people for all gifts within a fortnight of Christmas (or birthday).
- Sharing of ALL treat-based snacks with others.
- Giving to charity, however little, at every opportunity.
- Minding both your Ps and your Qs.
- Once your task is complete, offering to help others with theirs.
- Bearing minor inconveniences and slights with good grace.
- Brushing your teeth properly and flossing regularly.
- Treating all other people as if they are at least as worthy as yourself.

(For further examples, please consult your conscience.)

Perhaps if you could aim to tick items off this list, we might be able to fulfil your order, next year? In the interim, we wholeheartedly wish the best of luck to Mrs Abett.

Ever sincere,
Colin Elfsson
Senior Apologist

--*-*-*-*

Remember that Brussels sprouts are good for your elf!

From: A.Abett
To: enquiries@QualityPresents.co.fi
26/11/2000 10:01

Look, Legolas... or Dobby... or whatever your real name is... I'm tired of all of this condescension and time-wasting. Pretending to actually be Christmas Elves is a particularly childish way to behave, don't you think?

I didn't get where I am today without learning a thing or two about how to haggle for a deal.

Please either just let me know what extortionate price you would charge for expediting my offer... or forward my complaint directly to whomsoever calls themselves the boss of your unprofessional organisation.

Aidan

- - - - - - - - -

Junior Partner, Smann, Ropend and Abett
Sub-surface Seething in Style.

David Brown

From: QP-Co AutoMailBot
To: A.Abett@DingbatMail.co.uk
29/11/2000 11:47

Dear Slur or Madman

Please be informed that your email address
has been added to our 'blocked senders' list.

No further communications will be entered
into.

Merry Christmas

Love,
Santa
(The Boss)

--*-*-*-*

Once you've gone right to the top... you must either
go back or fall over the edge.

The gift you really need!

Santa's Quality Presents

🎁 1 😊 ✋

Bubbles
Be more fun and lively and social.

Fiddle
Get fit quick
Walk fast, then
start running
...

Night Owl
Stay up later!
Do you ever
find yourself
falling asleep too early?

Kitchen Scales

Amaryllis
Down to
Earth?
What if you

Sand Timer
Never quite
got enough
time?

2. A gift of time

"Mum?"

"Yes, Carrie dear?"

"When are you going to tell me why there are all of these sand timers on the shelf? There must be twenty of them."

"Twenty-one, actually." Alison looked up at the timers, counting them again, even though she did know precisely how many there were.

"Well? You did say that you would tell me when I got old enough."

"They were for Daddy."

After a pause. "But didn't he get them before he died?" The frankness of the young.

"No, dear. He did get them – and they were the second-to-best gift he ever had."

"Did you give them to him?"

"No, Uncle Mark and Auntie Kate did."

"But why would anyone need twenty-one sand timers?"

"Okay, Carrie, let's sit down and I'll tell you the whole story... at least as much as was told to me."

It was 1990, the year you were born. Your father was already very, very ill. We were worried that he wouldn't live long enough to see you born.

As part of our desperate scrabbling for any type of treatment, we found out about one place that might sell a treatment to keep him alive just a little bit longer. Someone had sent us an article they had found in a magazine. Unfortunately, the article mentioned that it was only available from a small town in Finland.

"Finland?" asked Carrie.

"Yes, up in the north - Lapland, to be specific."

I couldn't fly over there myself because I was within three weeks of giving birth to you, so I persuaded your Uncle Mark and Auntie Kate to go for me. You know, they're busy people, but they're amazing negotiators and we thought what I was asking them to do was going to be difficult.

Mark loved his brother and shared his pain and so they took some holiday and flew to Gällivare, in the north of Sweden, from where they would hire a car and drive across the border into Finland.

The day before they flew, the doctor had told us that your dad probably only had one more week to live – and that he'd be better cared for if he spent those days in hospital. He didn't want to, though; you were due in three weeks and he wanted to do as much as he could to prepare the house for you.

"Why was it going to be difficult?"

Well, they were flying to a place they'd never been to before, with a language different to any they had learnt... to try to buy some extra time for your father... for a patient who wasn't even there with them.

So, Dad and I (and you growing inside me, of course) stayed here while Mark and Kate flew away. It was only the early days of email... and texting hadn't been invented yet, I don't think. So, we couldn't keep in constant touch, like we do, these days. But they did phone me from Gällivare Airport. They'd been practising their Suomi phrases on me, like "lisäaika", meaning "extra time" and "kuinka paljon", "how much?"

"Suomi?"

"It's the Finnish word for Finnish... which must be the English word for Suomi, I guess?"

"Oh, so what's the Finnish word for word?"

"I don't know... let's look it up later.[1]"

It was September, which meant that winter was already beginning in that northern province. Mark and Kate were surprised at the crisp snow and cold winds, but moved quickly into their search. All they had with them to help was the small magazine article about the company they were looking for, called 'Quality Presents', which had been set up in an old toy factory.

Apparently, they got a few funny looks while asking around, but then a shop owner showed them an advert pinned up on her wall.

"What did it say?"

"I've got it here. I'll show it to you." Alison reached up to the top shelf and felt

---

[1] It's 'sana'.

around for an envelope that was sitting under the sand timers and a thin layer of dust. She pulled out some folded magazine pages and a small advertising card, which she showed to Carrie.

Laatu esittelee Santa.
Poro teollisuusalueelta.
Avata yhdestätoista
kello kolmeen.

It's in Finnish, but they got someone in their hotel to translate it for them. It says something like, 'Santa's Quality Presents – open eleven till three. Reindeer Trading Estate.'

They found it on the map. It would be a nice walk from the hotel, in the morning.

Ready for how late the sun set, so far north, they spent the evening in the hotel restaurant, overlooking the lakes. The locals were all very friendly – but refused to tell them anything else about what they were looking for. Although one of them went so far as to say that what they were looking for was 'only for locals'.

After a rare lie-in and a warming breakfast, they wrapped up snugly and headed out into the bright, icy land.

They had expected that it was going to be difficult to find someone to agree to meet with them… and were ready to endure several failed attempts. They spent the trudge through the snow revving each other up for a sustained effort and reached the Reindeer Trading Estate soon after eleven.

As they walked in from the cold and stamped the snow from their feet, there she sat: a woman with grey hair, rounded glasses and a large smile.

Her badge said 'Mary Claus' on it. "Nice touch," Mark whispered to Kate, with a smile.

They lifted out their English-Finnish dictionaries, ready for a hard negotiating session, gritted their teeth and smiled.

"Hei?" They said in Finnish. ("Hello.")

"Good afternoon," the kindly old woman said, in perfect but quaintly accented English.

"Oh, hello. I'm Mark. This is my wife, Kate. We would have phoned ahead but…."

"But we don't give out our phone number."

"No. That's a strange way to do business."

(Remember that Mark and Kate were in big business, back then – although they never did seem very happy at their work....)

"Well, you see, we are in a strange business," smiled the old lady. "I'm Mary. How may I help you?"

Kate got out the magazine article. She unfolded it and showed it to Mary as if proof were needed. Apparently, Mary was quite interested because she hadn't seen a copy before.

"Very nice," she said, after reading it carefully. "Although this sort of publicity is of little real use to us, as we don't sell our products abroad."

"No," said Kate, "that's why we travelled here to you."

"To see if you really do sell... intangible qualities?" Mark added.

Mary nodded and passed over a hand-typed catalogue, little more than a price list really. Mark and Kate read the first page in wonder.

SANTA'S QUALITY PRESENTS

Fiddle - as fit as...

Cat - got your tongue; learning not to speak

Bubble Juice - Bubbly personality

High-Vis Pants - for extra visibility, if you feel unnoticed

Night owl - to stay up late

Early Bird (catching worm) - to get up early

Sand Timer - for extra time

Inspiration - light bulb

"Well, yes, their objectifications, at any rate," she explained.

"Objectifications?" Kate's understanding of the word didn't apply to the concept, as far as she could see.

"Yes, we turn them into objects. We've been doing these for a while now, ever since Nick got fed up with the logistics of the old business and needed a change."

"Nick?"

"My husband... at first, you know, I thought he was having some sort of late-life crisis... but the locals really do seem to like what we do, nowadays."

"Um, so how long have you been in this particular business?" asked Mark.

"Well, since Nick tried to retire, wanted to pack it all in. It has taken two or three years to get it up and running... and we've been open for business in the local area for about two years now. I think we really knew we could be a success after we gave Judge Tuomari a set of 'fairness scales'. His judgements have never been so well respected."

"Is it... I don't really know how to ask this...," started Kate.

"Go on," smiled Mary.

"Your gifts – are they magical, in some sort of spiritual or religious way, or just amazingly high technology?"

"Does it matter?"

"Well, I don't know... does it?"

"People used to put all sorts of effort into trying to prove that Nick couldn't possibly deliver presents to every good child in the world in one night – but that didn't stop all of those children from knowing about his sleigh and reindeer, did it?"

It wasn't quite an answer, but Kate didn't know what else to say.

Still holding the amateurish catalogue, "And these qualities... they always work, do they?" Mark enquired, fascinated.

"Well, yes... but not always exactly as you'd expect. Judge Tuomari then bought his wife, Marja, some tolerance.

"Tolerance?"

"Yes, a spirometer to encourage you to take deep breaths... page three, I think?"

"And did it work?"

"Yes, well... at first, she was a little insulted at the gift and argued about it for hours, angry about how he had wasted his money – and that what he needed was a sense of proportion."

"Do you sell *that*?" asked Mark, amazed, flicking through the catalogue in search.

"No," laughed Mary. "That would be *really* unsafe. Anyway, the Judge eventually persuaded Marja to take it out of the box and give it a go... and now, she lets him go off hunting with his brothers whenever he wants to!"

"That's great P.R.," said Kate.

At this, Mrs Claus looked at her, as if with different eyes. "Yes, it's what led to the magazine article, indirectly... although publicity in a different country isn't very useful. Not all potential customers have your tenacity... or can pay the price we charge to buy some of their own! To be honest, I'm a little worried that our profits have dropped so much since changing business... but at least Nick is happy."

They laughed together, which Kate and Mark recognised as a good time to move their negotiations forward. "And the gift of time? How does that work?"

"Well, the timer takes one day to run its sand through... it gives you an extra twenty four hours, to do with as you will."

"Only a day? Well, okay... can we buy... all you have?"

"Oh, I'm sorry dear. But we only ever sell one at a time – and anyway, we only hold two dozen in stock."

"Well, can we buy two dozen, maybe... please? We really need to buy my brother another three weeks of life, so that he can see his daughter born."

"Oh, Mark," a tear almost formed in the corner of Mary's eye. "I really am so sorry but, as I said: we'll only sell one at a time. It's one of Nick's most firm conditions."

"*One* of his conditions? What are the others?"

"They're on the back... but I shouldn't complain. I often think that maybe I should get a little extra tolerance for myself?" Mary laughed a little before continuing. "Nick likes the idea of keeping the business on a small scale, but I confess that Mr Kolmikko, the Bank Manager, and I are both worried that his plans are on too small a scale. After overseeing an undertaking that was genuinely on a global scale, I am a little concerned that our new venture will either wither and die or become something other than what we wanted... possibly then even at risk of being taken over by someone with less than ideal motivation."

"And things like the 'no phone orders' and the 'local sales only' can only be restricting your profitability?" suggested Kate.

"And the limited sales – 'for good people only'," said Mark, referring again to the catalogue, "… 'only one item sold at a time'… are these completely necessary?"

"Well… maintaining our integrity is highly important, you know."

"Yes, but there must be some leeway. Do you really only sell by local order, as it says here? Why don't you accept email orders?"

"Well, I… to be honest, we don't have an elf who understands quite what email is. I'm not sure we can even get them, this far north?"

Kate ignored the elf reference and maintained her focus. "But you have got a phone line?"

"We have. Mainly for local use, though."

"Look," said Kate. "If we help you to get a phone modem and an email address…."

"…And help you to set up online ordering…" put in Mark.

"…Which will open up the whole world to you again, like before…."

"….Then… will you sell us all twenty four timers?"

"Well, I like the sound of it myself, but I'm really not sure that Nick would approve of email. It's all so, you know, *virtual*."

"But is it really any more so than sending your letters up a chimney?" Kate countered.

And so, they ended up leaving Lapland with the two full crates, 24 timers in all."

"Twenty-four? You said twenty one before."

"Yes... unfortunately, three broke in the baggage hold, on return."

"And that's why Uncle Mark and Auntie Kate are so happy now... working on this new international business."

"But they're not particularly rich from it, are they?"

"No, but they are very happily occupied."

Carrie looked up at the shelf of timers and thought about them for a few seconds.

"So, Mum, why weren't those timers the *best* gift that Daddy ever had?"

"Oh, my love, two days with you was."

Quality Proposal

Quality:

Superhero Powers
e.g. flight, heat vision, invisibility...

Totem / Objectification:

Superhero emblem T-shirts

Proposed by:

Pepper Minstix

Justification:

Think of how much better the world would be if people judged as 'good' could have superpowers... they would be sure to use them for good... and that's a good thing!

Decision:

Reason:

These don't exist – we can't make them. They are not personal qualities. Don't be silly.

Quality Proposal

Quality:

Intelligence

Totem / Objectification:

Shiny Button

Proposed by:

Colin Elfpoika

Justification:

This will give people an advantage e.g. in examinations and job interviews.

Decision:	Reason:
	We would rather support the development of tenacity and 'emotional intelligence' through empathy.

Quality Proposal

Quality:

Confusion

Totem / Objectification:

Dancing Lights

Proposed by:
Sylvia Elfsdotter

Justification:

One person may wish to confuse another
e.g.to distract from secretive deeds.

Decision:

Reason:

This is not the
behaviour of a good
person.

Quality Proposal

Quality:

Personal Wealth

Totem / Objectification:

Money Origami

Proposed by:

Alabaster Snowball

Justification:

An origami dragon represents the quality of being 'made of money', bestowing the recipient with all the money they could ever possibly want.

Decision:	Reason:
	Wealth is not a personal quality – it is a possession. Also, this could cause financial instability.

1. A Present for Santa

(Translated in entirety from the native Suomi.)

Harri Kolmikko checked his appearance in the mirror – tall and thin, clean shaven, tidy hair mostly turned now from black to grey, warm brown woollen suit.

This was a big day for Harri, a once-in-a-generation day.

He'd had a bad feeling about his ten o'clock meeting ever since it had been booked.

He sat there staring at the "Closure of Account" paperwork that sat on the desk in front of him in disbelief. He had managed the Claus family accounts for nearly twenty years, having taken on the responsibility from his own father.

Was he really going to be the one who lost his bank the business of Christmas, quite literally?

Harri quickly wrote the date onto the form as he waited. October 26th 1985.

Of course, he had read the historical files. He knew about the previous "wobbles". He understood the events which had led to them – and he thought he understood how each one had been navigated, allowing the accounts to stay open and the money to keep rolling through.

Nevertheless, he re-read his father's notes as he waited.

He was so distracted when Mr Claus came in from the snow, Harri almost didn't recognise him.

Obviously, people in town were well used to seeing him around, out of his 'uniform'. He only ever wore the red and white suit for special occasions. But today, he wore a non-descript grey suit and had trimmed his beard very short; he may even have lost some weight, recently?

The old man managed a smile as he sat down, shaking hands with Harri as usual.

"How are you, Harri?"

"Very well, thank you, sir."

"How's your wife?"

"Also well. She sends her regards."

"And young Laskin? Is he ready to take over the old family business yet?"

Harri caught himself wondering if he would even have a viable business, after today.

"Thank you for asking. He'll be finishing his professional qualifications next year... and is expecting to come and apprentice with us, after that."

"Expecting? Does he actually *want* to come and work here?"

Harri looked for a moment as if he didn't know how to answer that question. "Umm, well, I'm sure he thinks that it's the right thing to do."

"The right thing to do?" chuckled Mr Claus. "That could well be your family's motto, you know."

"I suppose so, but...."

"But what if he doesn't want to spend his entire adult life behind that brown desk, in this beige room... until his own son takes over from him?"

"What do you mean?" Harri looked around. Alright, it could maybe do with a lick of paint... possibly some new pictures of the local snowy spruce trees?

Lost in thought for a moment, he'd realised that Mr Claus was talking again, but that he'd missed the beginning of his sentence.

"...After year, you know? Always almost identical... the technology steps up a little each year... although the gratitude drops down." He took a deep breath and let it out again before speaking once more. "And so, Harri, it's time to call it a day." There. He had said it.

"A day?" Harri's instinct was to pretend that this wasn't really happening. But it was.

"I'm packing it in... this whole Christmas business. I'll sell it on, if anyone's fool enough to want it, but I don't honestly see why they would."

"But I...." Harri didn't get to finish his sentence. Santa was not to be interrupted.

"And so, I'm here to settle my final accounts."

Harri nodded, realised that he had subconsciously tidied the closure papers together, and spread them back out on the desk.

It was impossible not to like Santa – to empathise with him, to smile when he smiled and, today, to frown along with him. It was also impossible not to respect him, and his wishes.

The last thing Harri wanted was to cause conflict with a living legend, but he felt that he had to try to talk Santa out of his planned closure for the sake of his bank, as well as the health of the local economy, which depended so heavily on the toy factory... not to mention the spin-off merchandise, like the 'Santa Hats' and the ubiquitous 'Ho Ho Ho' signs. (He had always hated those, although he knew that they did actually make Santa laugh.)

"Of course. I have the paperwork here but, before you sign it, will you do me the favour of talking me through your decision? I had always thought you were happy in your work... you know... with that famous laugh of yours?"

Santa slowly removed his glasses and polished them with his thin grey woollen tie as he explained.

"It's more than one thing, you know. Letters have started to tail off... and it is getting increasingly difficult to identify 'good children'. Most people these days – they're so lacking in those important qualities – you know, like perseverance, empathy, fairness... I just don't like what the eighties are doing to us all."

Harri nodded, "But hasn't it always been this way? Isn't it just part of the human condition... you know... that none of us are as good as we should be?"

"Well, I'm pleased you noticed, Harri, it's certainly a trend our behavioural informetrics elf has identified. But it doesn't make me think any differently about the whole thing."

"And it's something I've always admired about you... your tenacity, your good-natured dedication... nothing to do with your other... abilities... you simply are a good person."

"Thank you," Santa smiled. "You do know how highly I prize being good. But do you know what I've noticed increasingly, over the last five years?"

"Tell me," nodded Harri.

"That presents *never* do any actual good... they *never* make life better... they *never* make people the slightest bit better. What does do good is meaningful interaction with family and friends... catching up, doing something with that special time to make each other's lives better. And, from another perspective, you know I'm increasingly concerned that the presents I deliver are rarely for adults... who do actually need them as much, you know... but are so much more difficult to get the right things for, you know."

Harri didn't know what to say to this. The older man's mood seemed to have suppressed his own determination.

"And, to be honest, Mrs Claus and I aren't getting any younger. We are planning to ride this twilight wave of ambivalence into retirement."

"But... what was it that pushed you to it? What made you decide to stop the delivery of presents?"

"Funny you should ask that... it was actually a gift from Mary."

"Mary?"

"Mrs Claus, you know?"

"I do," Harry smiled at the thought of the intelligent and perceptive woman. He had met her on many occasions, whether dealing with the day-to-day monetary issues of their global business, through their shared organisation of a sustainable local spruce forestry or bumping into her in the sleigh licensing queue. How could such a strong and committed member of the local community become the source of its economic collapse? "But, if I may ask... what was the gift that she gave you?"

Santa chuckled. "It was a trick light bulb!"

"A trick light bulb?"

"Yes, you know… you make a connection at the base with your wedding ring as you hold it and it appears to light up by magic."

"Why would she do that? Do you like magic tricks?"

Santa chuckled again. When he did this, it was impossible for Harri to just think of him as 'Mr Claus'… it wasn't the full 'Ho Ho Ho', but it was emphatically Santa sitting there. "No, Mary said it represented the… inspiration I needed – you know, to get out of this rut I've been in. Funny… it was the inspiration from the first Christmas presents, two thousand years ago, that set me off in the first place… how far they travelled to give their gifts. Although, I have always wondered what a baby would want with Myrrh, haven't you?"

"But it didn't work? The light bulb?" said Harri, trying to steer the old man back on track.

"Oh, no… you're mistaking me… it was as if it illuminated the entire world more brightly for me. I could see everything so much more clearly for the first time in… decades, possibly."

"Inspiration, eh?" muttered Harri. He didn't know whether he felt more amazed or beaten. "But it didn't make you feel more positive about your work again?"

"On the contrary: it inspired me to retire… to hang up the old red hat, put the old deer out to pasture, and begin to enjoy a very lazy retirement."

"The old dear?" Harri started. "She…."

"Rudolph and the gang – but you knew that really, didn't you?"

Harri tried to smile as Santa picked up the closure papers, shuffled them together, then reached for the pen.

He couldn't deny that Mr Claus's decision had come from the best of motives, but Harri didn't like the feeling of being beaten so he chose instead to express his amazement. "What a great present," he said, mostly to himself, "and actually a useful one."

"What?" Santa looked up. "What did you say?"

"I was thinking... your wife obviously has the same gift as you... the ability to bestow upon others a particular way of feeling, of being."

"Bestow?" frowned Santa. "I did always like that word! I was particularly sad to see it going the way of 'beverage'."

Harri didn't know what to say at this. However, he had noticed that Father Christmas had paused in his perusal of the documents. With quiet self-control, Harri sat on his hands, waiting for Santa to make the next move.

"Tell me, Harri," he looked up, thoughtfully, "what sort of quality would *you* most like to be given?"

"Well, I am already grateful to have been given both patience and a facility with accounting... I might say courage or bravery, but I do find *The Wizard of Oz* called to mind."

"What's that?"

"A film. You've never heard of it? But it's on the television every Christmas Day!"

"Oh, well, you'll understand I'm usually a little busy, just then."

"Of course, but... well it's basically about a search to gain the personal qualities the characters need... which they think the Wizard can actually give to them... like your 'inspiration'."

"And they gain these qualities, do they?"

"Yes, both through a shared adventure and then as actual gifts from the Wizard."

Mr Claus stared at him. He said nothing, but there were obviously deep thoughts swimming within. Or... was it almost as if a bulb had lit above his head?

Harri carried on talking, if only to delay the inevitable. "The Cowardly Lion is given a bravery medal... and the Scarecrow is handed a diploma to represent brains... although I prefer it in the original book where he was given pins to mix in with the sawdust stuffing in his head to make him 'sharper'." Harri saw that Santa's mouth was opening gradually; words were almost ready to come out.

Then, slowly at first, he began to speak. "You know, Harri, I'm going to have to go back home and talk all of this through with Mary, once more."

Harri asked the question he was dreading, but was professionally required to, "And the closure papers, Mr Claus?"

"I think I'd like to keep the old account open for now." And Harri realised that he was grateful to have been given the only gift he would have asked for.

As Santa tore the closure papers in half and stood to leave, Harri glanced around his tired old office. Maybe he would have to spruce it up a little before Laskin came back.

Perhaps he'd even put up one of those 'Ho Ho Ho' signs, to remind him of this day?

Quality Proposal

Quality:

Self-Restraint

Totem / Objectification:

Porridge Oats

Proposed by:
Sugarplum Mary

Justification:

We need a range specifically for those who haven't been good – to help them to be better.

Decision:	Reason:
	Interesting. We'll look to include this in the new range from 2020.

Quality Proposal

Quality:

Potential

Totem / Objectification:

Wunorse Opensleigh

Proposed by:

Alabaster Snowball

Justification:

Open the wrapping… and there's another wrapped parcel inside, saying "do not open… until you really deserve it".

Inside is another saying, "are you sure you really deserve it?"

…And then another…

Finally, just a small card saying "well done" – and it's enough.

Decision:	Reason:
	A great idea – leading the recipient towards their own gift.

Appendix A – Article from the "Slur on Sunday" Supplement Magazine

The Christmas gift you really need

Being a journalist only recently returned from Tiananmen Square, I'm something of a cynic... If you share this quality with me, do me the favour of putting aside your cynicism for a minute.

What would it look like, your cynicism, as you put it down? A little spade? Maybe a rusty knife? Just leave it there for now, if you will.

What if you could buy yourself the gift of more optimism? What would come in the box? A cloud with a silver lining? No, that could be too easily misunderstood.

A glass half-full – even worse... there are so many different views on what that represents. (Is it half empty? Is it both? Is it simply too big?)

Well, I found a place that will sell it to you as *rose-tinted glasses* – so you can see the good in everything.

Many of us are lucky enough to be living in a post-peak-stuff world. (You can thank Thatcher... if you've still got your cynicism suspended.) We're past the point where we actually *need* anything else. We've all read about the psychology experiments which show us that increasing the number of our possessions can't make us any happier.

And this makes shopping for Christmas presents increasingly difficult. We'll trawl the shopping centres or catalogues, recognising that anything we might buy will be either unnecessary or unwanted, if not both.

You can't buy happiness, of course... and we all learnt twenty years ago that money can't buy you love.

But what if you discovered that you could buy improvements to your own personal qualities? Personality upgrades, if you like.

What do you want to be given more of? Inspiration? Restraint? Empathy?

But who knows you well enough to buy it for you? What would you buy them?

A Finnish journalist, who I have known since we covered the Royal Wedding together in eighty-one, was given an 'early bird' (pulling an elasticated worm from the ground) and told me how she was suddenly able to get herself out of bed in the mornings... and managed to get so much more done each day.

(She later confessed to me that she had also given up binge drinking with other journalists, so I'm not entirely convinced that the test was fully fair.)

The bird, more importantly the quality that it represented, had come from a company calling itself, *'Santa's Quality Presents'*. Apparently they sell the locals all sorts of items representing these qualities... and the locals claim they actually work!

My friend even told me of the mother who had bought her university-age daughter the gift of an extra day to get her thesis complete for the deadline. Who'd have thought it? In this little old toy factory, near a reindeer farm, in northern Lapland... you could actually buy yourself more time!

I'd fly there and get some for myself... if I wasn't so busy!

Now... whether the gift really was imbued with magical powers or merely some kind of placebo influence, I don't know – but does it matter, as long as it works?

You can have your cynicism back now... would you like to have it gift wrapped?

Appendix B – Begging Questions

- What if someone got sent the wrong *Quality Present* by mistake? (Can too much inspiration be a bad thing?)

- What happens to a *Quality Present* when it's been finished with? Can they be passed on... or recycled... or do they just lose their magic?

- Can people swap their quality gifts? Can you take them back if you aren't satisfied with them?

- What if thieves once stole a shipment, which turned out to include boxes of 'honesty'? Would they all agree that they should return them, as soon as possible?

- What about the woman who bought her son faith – but he only ended up believing in himself?

- Wasn't there an attempt many years ago to package the original positive qualities – faith, hope, charity...?

- What if the Four Horsemen set up a rival service of negative qualities?

- What does Father Christmas do on Christmas Day, now? (What gifts is he given?)

- What place does Rudolph (and the rest of the Reindeer gang) have in the new organisation?

- Did you hear about the elves who, disgruntled with the changes to their T.O.C.s, broke away to form their own rival business?

- Aren't the qualities in this book all aimed at adults? What qualities would children want?

- Who bought Santa's old business from him? (How did that go?)

- How do people respond to the modern *Quality Presents* website, where the behavioural informetrics data graphs as a swingometer as you fill in the information?

Maybe we'll try to answer some of these questions in the future?

Appendix C – Commercialism and Charity

If you'd like to give this book to someone else as a "Quality Present", you can find it on LULU.com[2], along with some of my other stuff.

I'll pass on any profits to **Comic Relief**

(...so I can tick that off on Colin's List)

---

[2] NOT lulu.co.uk... that's a *very* different place!

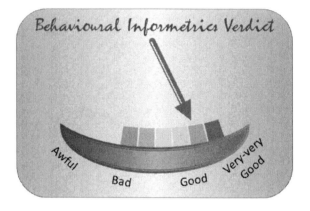

Printed in Great Britain
by Amazon